CREEPER CEEPERS

The Haunting of Grey Cliff Manor

Author
D.A. Wysong

22MusesPublishing.com

THE HAUNTING OF GREY CLIFF MANOR

Book One

D.A. Wysong

CHAPTER ONE-

TRUMAN

When Truman arrived at Grey Cliff Manor, he was taken back at how dreary and gloomy his new boarding school was. The huge, towering manor sat on top of one of the highest points of upstate New York. It overlooked both the Hudson River and Atlantic Ocean. The waves crashed up against the high cliff, giving off an eerie feeling. Being that he was already quite nervous, it made him feel even more alone.

His parents both worked abroad and quite often they were both away. Being an only child, they decided it was best for Truman to attend a preparatory school. The only consolation was that his cousin Renton would be attending this year. Though his cousin had younger brothers, his parents too, were away working as well. This was the first year the boys would be a way from their families.

Truman's parents couldn't be there to see him get settled in. Instead, their chauffer Miles was sent to accompany him on his journey to Grey Cliff. The drive was not so bad. It was about a two-hour drive from

Truman's stately home nestled nicely in the region known as the New York Harbor. Miles was quite handy, and a great asset to the De Lancey family.

Truman was used to being escorted by Miles since he was a young boy. He drove him to school and his musical lessons. There was even a time Truman took soccer lessons. Miles was a constant in his life and was there to help him get settled into his new home away from home. Truman was quite accustomed to the finer things in life. In fact his parents sent him on his way in the family's best car, the Bentley.

Truman's sandy brown hair was blowing all around in the fierce gusts of wind coming from the ocean. He squinted his cool green eyes as he peered over at the desolate grey waters crashing against the cliff. He breathed a deep sigh and most certainly concluded that Grey Cliff Manor was very creepy.

He grabbed his luggage and he and Miles walked up to the entrance. There standing was a frail old man. His skin was quite pale, and his hair was white as snow. He had a scowl on his face with grey piercing eyes. He was also dressed proper, just as a Headmaster should be. Truman tried not to think of the proper attire he would have to endure while attending school there.

Truman walked into the foyer where a grand, quite long staircase stood. The grandeur of the staircase took precedence over the stately room. Huge chandeliers were hanging from above, but still the room was dimly lit. The windows were covered in stained glass, such as a church. The room was stuffy and musky and dim, and Truman did not even want to think about how he would endure this place until Thanksgiving break. He sighed a deep sigh and followed both the Headmaster and Miles up the staircase to get settled into his new home away from home.

CHAPTER TWO

NANA

Truman stood looking out the window of his room. He was on the top floor of the manor and his room was in the part of the manor referred to as the tower section.

Grey Cliff Manor was equipped to house one-hundred fifty boys from all around the world. The prestigious preparatory school was designed to educate and equip boys from wealthy families to the standards of higher learning while preparing them for expected duties once they reached maturity. This is what his parents told him when they informed him he was being carted off to Grey Cliff.

The only solace Truman felt he had was that his cousin, Renton, would be there as well. Although they hadn't seen one another since they were about eight years old, he had fond memories of their time together. The two of them played together at their grandmothers' estate. They had stayed there with their Nana for an entire summer.

Nana was what she wanted us to call her, however, that name was breaking all the rules of proper etiquette. Looking back at his rather rigid childhood, those memories were some of Truman's fondest memories.

Her estate sat on eighty-three acres of rolling hills and a private beach set on the Atlantic Ocean. The two boys were given riding lessons and would often ride horses with Nana.

Once they even got to experience being a party to fox hunting. They met the headmaster of the foxhounds, and it was quite a sight to watch the social ritual that their Nana was so very fond of.

The two boys would play tag and sip lemonade on the terrace with Nana. She was quite a delight. Although she came from a family of great prominence, she was a free spirit. She would laugh and tell her funny tales of growing up a young girl on that very estate.

We would sit and listen to her funny torrid tales with pure delight, while eating our favorite French Danish treats. She was the greatest storyteller that Truman had ever known. When she spoke, it was as though she would capture you. It felt like you were there with her in a different time and era.

Sitting on the edge of his bed, Truman felt a cool breeze blow against his neck.

Goosebumps appeared and he could not shake the feeling that someone was there in the room with him. He tried to shake the feeling off.

He looked around at the gloomy faint lit room and stared at what would be Renton's bed across from his. He had quickly unpacked when he arrived. He was taught early on to do what needs to be done and be fully prepared. Now that he had everything in order, he was ready for the day.

He was quite excited about the arrival of his long-lost cousin, Renton. Now he was just waiting for Renton's arrival, he looked down at his watch. Within the hour his cousin

would be arriving.

CHAPTER THREE

RENTON

The dining room was quite large as Truman glanced around the expansive room. The theme seemed to heighten a lot of décor accents in hues of red and gold. There were about twenty large round tables with wooden back chairs circled around the room. The uniforms that were imposed on the boys made everything look that much more formal. Truman was used to this of course. He blended away into the uniformity of his surroundings.

While in line he gracefully chose his lunch for the day. Broccoli cheddar soup and a nice grilled cheese sandwich seemed a perfect comfort food for the day. He looked around as he searched for a friendly face to sit down next to. The room had but a few boys eating in it. He thought it was probably due to late arrivals for the new school year. Instead, he just sat alone, eagerly eating his delicious soup and sandwich.

Sipping his soup, he looked up to see his cousin Renton standing there. Renton was towering over him as though he was a huge oak tree.

"By God, Renton you have gotten huge," exclaimed Truman.

"Yet, it seems you have only grown a bit," Renton replied. Truman stood up and hugged his cousin eagerly. He was so glad to finally see a familiar face. Both the boys laughed, and Renton hurriedly got in line for some lunch as well. Renton of course received a double helping of soup and was offered two grilled cheese sandwiches due to his stature and presence. The two boys enjoying their lunch were laughing and talking. It was just like when they were eight years old again, old friends and the best part was that they are family. Truman began to think maybe it wouldn't be so bad here anyway.

The lights began flickering as the two boys sat and devoured their lunch together. Lightening lit up the dining hall as the rain began to patter against the huge windows. The eeriness of the manor never seemed to quit, Truman thought as he sat there.

"Did you see that?" asked Truman.

Renton not blinking an eye absorbed in eating his soup and sandwich, did not bat an eye.

"What?" asked Renton.

"The lights," softly replied Truman.

"It was just the storm," said Renton. The two boys finished eating together and cleaned up after themselves.

They made their way up the statedly staircase and headed to their room for Renton to get settled in. Climbing the staircase Truman heard a soft whisper of his name. He looked over at Renton, oblivious to anything. The lights continued to flicker even in foyer. It seemed that Truman might be just imagining every little thing around him in the creepy old manor that he would call his home for the next year.

Just as the boys arrived at the top of the staircase Renton toppled over losing his balance. He fell back several steps, taking his breath away. Cold air encircled Truman leaving the hair on his arms standing straight up. Confused and worried, Truman turned around to help his cousin.

Renton looking devastated, scowled at Truman yelling, "Why did you go and do that?"

"Do what," questioned Truman, his voice shaking.

"Push me," screamed Renton.

Truman stumbling for words said, "But I didn't push you."

One of the school masters Richard, scurried up the stairway to nervously ask what happened.

"He stumbled back," Truman spoke hurriedly.

"More like I was pushed," exclaimed Renton.

The school mastered peering over at Truman questioned them again. Renton hesitated and then said, "No, I fell back and lost my balance."

The two boys hung their heads down and the school master helped Renton hobble down the long and winding staircase. Truman followed behind feeling numb from what had happened. They arrived at the foyer where a nurse came and escorted Renton into the infirmary. The school master began to take notes of what exactly happened to file a report just to have on file. Truman oblivious to what the school master was asking him couldn't help but notice the faint trace of a shadow of a man at the top of the staircase. Why couldn't anyone else see what he was seeing? Why could no one else feel what he was feeling?

Dread filled Truman as he made his way back up to the stairwell to his creepy room.

CHAPTER FOUR

COUSINS

Renton arrived back at his bedroom that he shared with his cousin. He only arrived with the help of some crutches. Having a sprained ankle was never fun and knowing that your cousin was the cause of it was doubly not fun. Renton was a bit salty about the fact that Truman would do such a thing. He could not understand why he would do such a thing. The two boys hadn't seen one another for over five years, and when they were reunited in the dining hall, it was like they had never been apart.

Renton hopped onto his bed looking around at his disarray of luggage and belongings that he still had to unpack. Truman was laying his bed in the dimly lit room. Peering over his covers he watched Renton climbing into his bed.

Silence filled the air as the two boys locked eyes. Truman looked away, embarrassed because he knew that Renton thought he pushed him down the stairs. Why would Renton ever think he would do such a thing? Wondered Truman.

"I know it had to be an accident," Renton said. Truman looked up desperately hoping that Renton would believe what he was about to say. "I swear it wasn't me."

"Then who was it?" retaliated Renton

"A ghost," Truman said rather abruptly.

"A ghost?" echoed Renton

"Yes, a ghost!" replied Truman again.

"Whatever," dismissed Renton, now being irritated.

"If this is how it's going to be I'm going to ask to be moved into another room."

"Please don't do that!" Truman was distressed. "Something really doesn't feel right here.

I keep getting cold chills, and I keep seeing glimpses of something moving fast out of the corner of my eye. You'll see! Just give it another day or so. Please don't be mad at me, it really was not me who pushed you," he insisted.

Truman was looking at Renton pleading while locked onto Renton's eyes, hoping that he would somehow believe him.

"I believe you Truman." Renton spoke softly.

"I know it was not you who pushed me down the steps. You couldn't have, you were beside me. Someone pushed me from the front. I don't understand because there was no one there, besides us on the staircase. Nothing human that is," said Renton with a trembling voice.

Truman was alarmed at what he was hearing his cousin say and at the same time relieved that he believed him.

The two boys sat sitting across from each other looking at one another in disbelief. Truman broke the awkward silence, "Now what?"

"I don't know," replied Renton. "Hopefully it just never happens again, and it was a freak incident."

Truman sighed & chuckled, because he doubted that it will all just go away.

"I don't know if I even believe in ghosts," Renton said under his breath.

Truman spoke up, "Yet here we are, having you pushed down the staircase and having a sprained ankle."

The boys just seemed to shrug it all off and decided to call it a night. Renton dimmed the lamp to snuggle under the covers, plumping his pillows up nice and fluffy while trying to get comfortable for the night.

Truman spoke out into the darkness and

announced that in the morning he would help

Renton get settled in from packing. Renton

nodded his head yes as he drifted off to sleep.

Truman was tossing and turning. He

could not get comfortable. The moonlight

shined brightly through the window. He could

see the shadow of the big oak trees moving

back and forth. The limbs of the tree

scratched against the windows, and the wind

was howling thru the cracks of the window.

He could feel a cold draft blowing through.

He was not convinced that it was indeed the

wind, or rather it was a spirit or ghost of sorts

lingering near him as he dared not to move in his bed, pretending to sleep. His eyes now closed afraid to open them for fear of what he might see. He managed to doze off to sleep, but was abruptly woke in a dead silence.

Over in the corner of the boy's room sat a pale white lady dressed in a flowing white gown. She was rocking in the chair methodically. Back and forth watching the boys sleep. Hovering outside the window were two spirits that slipped in through the window cracks. The spirits fixated on the two boys. One spirit stood silently looking down at them. He was dressed properly with the finest of silks, like that of an old aristocratic man with slicked back hair and long mustache. He stood there staunchly for what seemed a lifetime. Truman's heart was beating so fast and loud that he was afraid that the spirits could hear it. Frozen with fear, Truman tried as hard as he could not to whimper.

When he didn't think it could get any worse the doorknob began to turn. The door creaked and a faint light appeared from a flashlight. Standing there next to the door was the school master checking in and making his rounds. The school master Richard was a tall slender man, in his mid-forties. He seemed to be a quiet and understanding man. Right at this moment Richard's presence was greatly appreciated.

To Truman's surprise the two spirits has disappeared. Not knowing why they all disappeared, the fact that they were gone gave him some relief. They were beginning to make Truman very uncomfortable. Being very anxious and tired, he tried to put it out of his mind as he finally drifted off to sleep. The wind was once again howling through the cracks of the window. The moonlight shined into the boy's room, and the faint smell of a rose parfum lingered in the air.

CHAPTER FIVE

THE APPLETONS

Francis and Fanny Appleton-Grey were a family of great prominence. Their family estate that stood on the highest peak of the Hudson Valley screamed loudly that they were leaving their mark on this community.

Francis Appleton-Grey was a shrewd and prominent businessman. He was well versed in trade and commerce, although he specialized in both the forestry and iron trade. That was his specialty; however, Francis would venture into whatever he could gain the most from when it came to business. He was known for his mean streak and very few men would dare to come up against him when it came to setting the record straight for business dealings. Mr. Appleton-Grey always had the last say.

Mrs. Appleton-Grey on the other hand was an impartial lady full of grace and kindness. She upheld her duties with fairness and dignity, always. She was known for her lavish parties and was loved by all who knew her. Her servants were graced by her presence, and she made sure that they were taken care of with the best clothing, food and lodging. She tried to always follow her husband's wishes and was always benevolent to children; however, Francis seemed to not be pleased with Fanny when she gave birth to a child of her own. Eventually she had not one, but two children.

First was a boy, Edward. He modeled after his father Francis. He seemed to be a bit callus as a child, you could say he had a mean streak. He was the first born and as he grew up in this family of prominence, he quickly adapted the thought that he was very entitled. He was known for treating everyone with unfairness wherever he would go. Edward was just eight years old years when his sister Elizabeth was born.

When Fanny was graced with a beautiful baby girl whom the Appleton's named Elizabeth, the two were nearly inseparable. Right from the beginning, Elizabeth barely made it into this world. She was born very frail and had to have extra care. Elizabeth had the spirit of an otherworldly being. She was tiny in build, fragile and pale, with blue eyes and long flowing blonde hair. When she was not ill, she would run in the open fields, when weather allowed her to do so. She would befriend the woodland creatures in the huge estate and loved to be close to nature. With her alignments however, the fragile little Elizabeth was confined mostly to the quarters of Grey Cliff Manor.

Towards the end of Elizabeth's short life, she would sit in her tower room, looking out the window longing to be frolicking in the open fields. She missed sitting by the ocean side filled with sea gulls and the wonderful smell of the salt air.

No one could have ever imagined that young Elizabeth would have fallen to her death from the very cliff of Grey Cliff Manor that her grandfather had built. She was just barely six years old when she died. All the money in the world and all the riches that the

Appleton-Grey Family had acquired would never compensate for the loss of their beautiful young daughter. Mr. Appleton-Grey, as staunch and stern as he was to the world, could hardly cope with the loss of their daughter. Seeing his beautiful wife Fanny in mourning was hard to watch. She deteriorated slowly and eventually died of a broken heart. Edward however seemed to thrive even stronger and more troublesome as he grew up a harsh demanding man.

Grey Cliff Manor was once was a hub of great music, joy and jubilee soon became a place of dark sadness. After the death of Elizabeth there was never another party held in the grand estate of Grey Cliff Manor. Eventually Francis Appleton-Grey passed away and the only remaining person was Edward, was now a young and prominent businessman. He like his father was very shrewd. Now controlling the family business and the sole heir, was quite wealthy. The difference between him and his father was that Edward was not only shrewd but ruthless in his business dealings. Some would call him outright dangerous.

As the years went by Mr. Edward Appleton -Grey never did marry. He did seem to leave a trail of ladies of prominence all broken hearted with torrid tales to tell of his ruthlessness. There was even one lady that was never seen again and there were whispers that Edward had his hand in her disappearance. No one ever really investigated this tragic event. Some speculated it was because she came from a family of unimportance. She was a mere commoner, and no one dare to anger Mr. Appleton-Grey. The police just made a report of the disappearance and that was the end of her story.

Edward Appleton died all alone in the library of his grand estate Grey Cliff Manor. Though he was quite wealthy he had dwindled down to just a handful of servants.

The manor needed repairs from the weather and elements being on top of the cliff.   What was once a manor of grandeur, joy, and stature was now a gloomy and crumbling old manor.

One cold November morning, one of the servants found Edward Appleton slouched in his favorite chair. A glass of scotch sat nearby, and a throw blanket covered the man. The fireplace had died out. With no warmth in the room, it gave off a feeling that it would never be warm in that house again.

CHAPTER SIX

GHOSTLY COLLISION

The sunlight was piercing through the dark bedroom of the tower where Truman and Renton were bunkered down. Truman who was awake, looked over at his cousin Renton who was stirring. He grunted a bit, probably due to the sprained ankle he had received the day before. Truman scouting all the disarray of Renton's belongings knew what the two of them would be doing most part of the morning. It was Sunday and they had one more day before their academics would soon take precedence.

Jumping out of bed Truman grabbed his clothes and soon got dressed. Renton now awake, joined in hurriedly getting dressed. The two boys dug in and quickly put away all of Renton's clothes and belongings into the dressers and closets.

The two then joined in with the rest of the boys for breakfast. The dining room was filling up rather nicely. Everyone seemed to have arrived and they were now at full capacity. The soft chatter of conversation as well as excitement filled the air. Later in the day they would all meet up for a game of soccer. It was a beautiful September day full of sunshine and a mild breeze coming from the ocean. Renton of course would not be able to play soccer, but he would be the scorekeeper. It was a job that he seemed to look forward to pursuing.

The two boys went outside and sat near the garden. The huge estate was surrounded by a large line of towering trees of great proportion and a dense forest followed deep within. On the other side was the Atlantic Ocean. Grey Cliff Manor sits on top of a huge cliff overlooking the ocean. Dare not to get too close to the edge for the drop was deadly, six hundred feet straight down. The landscape was filled with rough and jagged rocks and boulders. Though it was the ocean, the temperatures were on the cold side even in the summer months, not to mention the sharks that the ocean was known for in this region. Looking down from the cliff the waves crashed harshly against the jagged rocks.

Truman was ready for the upcoming game of soccer. He hadn't played much football since last season. His family traipsed around different parts of Europe most of the previous summer. One of the things he loved about sports was the interaction of the other kids. Being an only child had its advantages but had disadvantages as well. The main disadvantage as far as Truman was concerned is it was a lonely place. He had grown accustomed to being alone and occupying his time with extracurricular activities such as sports, music and learning foreign languages. He spoke both French and German fluently and was also learning Spanish. His father directed him this way to ensure his place of prominence and diversity in the family business. His father was an entrepreneur of sorts and had a knack for the stock markets. Speaking multiple languages made his fortune all that more lucrative.

As Renton sat uncomfortably on the hard bench near the gardens, something caught his eye. Along the tree line it seemed that something moved quickly. His peripheral vison caught something once again that was quite odd. He was certain that he seen a white floating image passing the entrance of the forest. He took another glance, and nothing was there. It seemed odd to see something moving over there because no one ever seemed to want to venture out into the forest. From what was rumored it was a forest that was quite dense, and easy to get lost. It was said that many years ago a young boy wandered off into the forest never to return. A search party was organized and the group of men looked for the young boy. He wasn't found until days later where he apparently was frozen to death. It was a local tragedy that shook the town and seemed to impact everyone. From then on, no one had wanted to enter the forest.

"I could have sworn I seen something along the tree line. Just as sure as I thought something was there, it seemingly disappeared," he mumbled as though talking out loud to himself. Truman noticed Renton looking along the tree line. He sat up and began casing the area in search of what his cousin could have possibly seen. Nothing appeared to be out of the ordinary, but Truman could also not shake the feeling that something or someone was watching them. He had this feeling ever since Miles drove him up the long winding driveway. He shook it off then as though he was just nervous arriving to his new home away from home.

Truman played wholeheartedly the afternoon's game of soccer. Renton kept score, and it was a very pleasant Sunday afternoon at Grey Cliff Manor Preparatory School. It was beginning to feel as though there was a sense of brotherhood. It was no longer just a bunch of boys all thrown together to become the men that their families expected them to be.

Later that evening after leaving the dining hall the two boys ventured to look around the Manor. It was quite vast in size, and one could easily get lost if they weren't careful. Down the corridor past the dining hall was the old library. There were a lot of books that were both old and new. They updated the library where there were individual tables with desk lights and computers so the boys can study at their own discretion. Truman's eyes lit up when he saw the collection of books as he entered the library. Renton also was excited to see all the books in the history section. This was his forte. He loved reading about the past and how everything plays out along certain timelines. He was a history buff that was for sure. Truman on the other hand loved to read about things unknown or yet to be explored. The two boys were mesmerized by the pure existence of all that was inside the 4 walls of this extraordinary library.

There was even a sliding ladder to climb up to the top shelf and read until your hearts content. There was a special section entitled midway up the bookshelves under the name of Grey Cliff Manor. This caught the attention of both the boys. The school master came up from behind them declaring that it was time to retire to their rooms for the night. After all, the next morning was the first day of school and it was important to get settled in for a good night's rest. The two boys followed Richard's instruction and made their way back to the foyer. Renton wobbled up the stairs with his crutches though he was coming along rather nicely as far as his ankle was concerned. It was a simple sprain and with proper care he would be as good as new in no time. Renton was still a bit nervous when reaching the top but made his way safely. Truman followed up behind him unbeknownst to Renton, wanting to safeguard his cousin from further injury.

The boys dressed for bed and washed up. They both laid their uniforms out to be ready for the next morning. Books and back packs were all geared up and they couldn't help but be excited for a new school year.

The two boys chatted a bit before Renton drifted off to sleep. He snored a bit which was going to be something Truman had to get used to. After all it would be an entire year that they would be bunking together.

Truman tossed and turned trying to get comfortable. He was quite sickened about the night before and the ghostly visitor that appeared at his bedside. His thoughts began to wander about why this could have possibly happened. The winds were picking up once again, howling softly outside the window. The full moon light was shining very brightly through the rickety windows almost blinding Truman in the very dark room. He suddenly felt a very cold chill in the air once again. Though it was drafty, this was not a draft. Goosebumps appeared all over him and he feverishly sat straight up in his bed. A moaning began, at first softly and then very loudly. He just couldn't believe Renton was sleeping through all this ruckus. Over to the far corner of the room a rocking chair began rocking softly. Back and forth steadily, it continued to rock and creak softly. He could swear he smelled his Nana's perfume in the air lingering. There for a minute he thought he could see his Nana. He was certain of it.

Just as Truman looked away from the rocking chair, there stood the tall pale ghostly man with the stiff curved mustache. His eyes were black, and he had a sinister scowl on his face. Truman screamed as this ghostly force was literally inches away from him. The ghostly man just laughed and laughed. His once darkened room was now a room filled with old furniture and a lady hovering over a small frail little child. The woman was weeping, and the child lay limp. She was bruised and her hair was wet with seaweed entangled in it. There was a boy standing along the shadows of the room watching intently as he too had a scowl on his face. Along the wall crept a dark shadow of a man. No face just an outline of a man, nothing but blackness.

Truman rubbed his eyes with disbelief, and he couldn't believe what he was seeing! Was he dreaming or was this really happening? It made no sense and just as fast as it happened it was all gone. Truman wondered why was he the only one that was seeing hearing and feeling these odd things? Why was this happening? Was he going mad? He felt frightened and very anxious about what was happening to him. Who was that scary ghost that kept appearing at his bed side? Who was the strange boy who was lurking in the shadows? Why was there a little girl covered in seaweed and a woman crying over her? Truman's thoughts were going a mile a minute as he tried to sort it all out. He was going to have to find answers. Where could he find the answers? It wasn't like he could ask the school master or anyone for that matter. He tried comforting himself with the thought that he would go in search of answers. He was trying to be analytical about such matters which was going to be quite the challenge. Nothing seemed to make sense.

Nothing about this entire situation had any

logic to it.

CHAPTER SEVEN

GHOSTLY ENCOUNTERS

Renton lay fast asleep as the covers were slowly being pulled down by an invisible force. There was a cold chill in the air, and he tried pulling his blankets up over him. To his dismay there were no covers on his bed. He was still groggy as he wrestled his blankets up from the floor. He knew that he would be waking even earlier than the previous day. Tomorrow morning would be with the first day of school at Grey Cliff. He looked at the alarm clock and it was just 3am.

He glanced over towards Truman and his blankets were also on the floor.

He wrestled back and forth, trying to get comfortable. He could not believe how cold it was in the room, now he could even see his breathe. He shuddered from the cold and finally got wrapped back up in his little cocoon of covers. He noticed the curtains moving a bit from the draft from the window. You could always hear the howling of the wind at Grey Cliff. It never seemed to really stop because of the constant ocean breeze.

There was an unsettling air about the place though he never mentioned it to

Truman. He would think that Renton was just being a baby. They were thirteen years old now and such childish fantasies of haunted places needed to be put away. Renton always had a rather active imagination, or so his parents always said. Maybe it was the fact that he read so much and often wrote stories about what ifs. He didn't share this often with many others. In fact, he didn't share it with anyone. Late at night he would just write in the privacy of his own thoughts and fall off to sleep.

Besides the eeriness of Grey Cliff, the fact that he was laying here with a sprained ankle and he knew it wasn't Truman's fault.

He also knew it was deliberate, and that there was no one else around. That meant just one thing, and that one thing was indeed that it was a ghost who pushed him. Renton had never heard of a ghost getting physical with people. Then again, he never really read much about the subject of ghosts or ghostly encounters. However, he did do a lot of reading about history. It just so happens that historical stories can be some of the most haunted stories to tell. The tales of Bluebeard or the Canterbury Ghost were quite scary. One of the scariest stories that Renton thought of when it came to ghost stories was Charles Dickens, The Ghost of Christmas Past. It was very frightening to think of a ghost from your past to come back and haunt you.

Renton tried to get the thoughts out of his brain of hauntings and ghost stories. He was a bit scared of the staircase due to being pushed down. Just as he was about to drift off to sleep, the door began to creak. The doorknob began to turn slowly, and the door began to open. He tried to close his eyes to pretend he was asleep, but he peeked for he wanted to see who or what was on the other side of the door. Or did he?

There standing near his bed was a boy of about the same age. His clothes were a bit odd with knickers and a vest. He dressed as though he was from a different period of time. He recognized the clothing from reading history. Probably from around the mid 1800's. Very strange indeed he thought to himself, trying to remain calm. The boy continued to stand near him, and Renton didn't know how much more he could take of lying perfectly still. What in the world does he want? Just as fast as he appeared he vanished. Renton now startled, got up and woke Truman up to tell him he had just seen a ghost.

He was shaking his cousin wildly until he awoke. Truman sat straight up rubbing his eyes, and the two boys completely went frozen as the strange ghostly woman appeared

right before their eyes. She stood there in a

long white dripping wet gown. She just stood

there weeping, and weeping. She was

inconsolable like she would cry for an

eternity. She was pale with long brown

flowing hair, and water was dripping all

around her. Seaweed was all over the floor

and the smell of the ocean was strong in the

air. An older gentlemen stood behind her very

stern and very solemn. His face was

expressionless unlike the weeping woman.

Just then the rocking chair in the far corner

began to gently rock. Back and forth, back

and forth the chair continued to rock. The

solemn ghostly gentleman raised his hand and began to point outside the window. The woman continued to just weep, now holding a small young child. It was a little girl with long blonde hair, tangled with seaweed. Her body was badly bruised, and her dress was ripped to near shreds. Her body lay limp in the woman's arms.

A low growling began to surface from within the closet door, as it began to crack open all by itself. Deep within the closet you could see piercing though the darkness red glowing eyes and the continued snarl and low growling got louder and louder. The ghostly figures of the weeping lady the child and the solemn man disappeared. The only thing left was the growling and the red eyes. The two boys were frozen in fear, as they just sat there unable to move.

The bedroom door opened and there stood the school master Richard making his rounds. He immediately noticed the boys up and petrified with fear. He ran over to see if they were alright. He switched the desk light on and broke the silence.

"Is everything alright here?" Richard exclaimed, sounding frightened himself.

The boys mustered a "Yes," in harmony as they both chimed together.

Renton still a bit frozen with fear, was pointing at the closet. Truman exclaimed that they had just witnessed seeing a ghost.

"It was a ghost, or a spirit or something that was not human. It was the most frightening thing I have ever seen," he said quickly again while trying not only to convince Richard but himself.

Richard stood there in silence listening to the boys jabber on with what they had just encountered. Richard paused and looked around the room nervously. He continued to speak to the boys. With what he was telling them, they just could not believe their ears.

Richard told the boys of the history of Grey Cliff Manor. He shared with them the tragedy of the Appleton-Grey family and how their young child of a tender age of just six years old, fell to her death off the cliff and drowned. How the mother Fanny died soon after of a broken heart and how Francis Appleton Grey became a recluse. He lived alone for years after the tragedy and too died later in about mid age, and the only living son Edward carried the family legacy on never to be married. He too died here at the house in his very old age.

He went on to tell them the locals rumored that Edward Appleton-Grey was a heartless man and rumor had it that he had to do with the disappearance of a local woman, never to be found. The townspeople were afraid of Edward and never really pursued the matter. Some years later a young boy of one of the servants wandered off into the woods, days later he was found frozen to death.

"So much heartache," said Richard as he hung his head down.

There are those who hear strange noises here in the tower. Some even see the ghostly apparitions. It is here, in this part of the tower where the young child resided in her bedroom. She was a sickly child. It was also in this very tower that Mrs. Appleton-Grey lived her last days as she died of a broken heart.

"What about the boy?" asked Truman.

"Who is the boy?" questioned Renton.

"I would imagine that might have been the boy lost in the woods," replied Richard. The boys proceeded to tell Richard that the boy was about their age. He was about thirteen or so and wearing clothes like that of the mid 1800's. Renton was convinced it was not the young boy in the woods.

"I don't know of any other children it could be other than what I told you. You might have a look at the books in the library downstairs," said Richard.

Richard continued to encourage the boys to read the few books on the Appleton-Grey family and the history of Grey Cliff Manor. Richard turned around and turned the lights out reminding them that morning would be coming sooner than later. He walked out and shut the door.

Renton and Truman drifted off to sleep out of pure exhaustion and knowing at least part of why the ghostly encounters were happening. Renton was fast of sleep snoring loudly and as Truman drifted off to sleep, he wondered what the apparitions were trying to tell them. What was it that Mr. Appleton-Grey was pointing at? Tomorrow they would begin to find the answers.

CHAPTER EIGHT

YOUNG EDWARD

Morning came way too early, as the boys began getting ready for their first day of academics at Grey Cliff. They dressed in their uniforms and grabbed their backpacks. They headed down to the dining hall for breakfast. Renton was managing now without crutches, but he still had to take his time getting around with his now bruised ankle. The two boys ate their oatmeal and blueberry bagels wholeheartedly. They downed their juice and made a mad dash for their first class which was algebra.

The first day of school went by quickly and before they knew it, they were back in their rooms changing into something more comfortable. The two of them knew that as soon as classes were over, they were heading to the library but not for studying academics rather to read up on the history of Grey Cliff and the Appleton-Grey family. It was fortunate for Truman and Renton that the two boys loved to read. This library was a gold mine of books, and they couldn't wait to see what their researching would reveal.

Renton climbed up the ladder to the bookshelf. He pushed his way towards the section of Grey Cliff Manor. He scanned the few books that read Grey Cliff and grabbed the two best books he could find. He climbed back down the ladder and made his way over to the table that Truman had saved for them. Truman opened one book and Renton opened the other. They boys began skimming through the pages when Renton suddenly stopped, fixated on a page in the book. His face grew pale, and Truman became concerned, Renton turned the book around and showed Truman the picture of the boy. A young Edward when he was about their age. The very ghostly apparition the two just seen the night before. Truman's face drained of color and the two boys just stared at one another.

There in the pages of the history of Grey Cliff was a picture of Edward just thirteen at the time of his young sister's death. It was the day of the funeral and there stood beside him his beautiful young mother Fanny, and his father Francis. The two boys were both perplexed, why would Edward be appearing as a boy? Why would the apparition of the solemn gentleman be pointing toward the window? The ocean side was near the tower window. So, what could this be all about?

The two boys jotted down the notes and made a copy of what the young Edward looked like just for reference. This puzzle was quite perplexing indeed.

Truman while in the library googled information about ghostly apparitions, hauntings, and on how to make it all stop.

"There has to be a reason why these apparitions are revealing themselves to us," Truman exclaimed.

"There has to be a reason why young Edward is lingering behind them when they appear," retorted Renton. The boys agreed that they needed to figure out just what was going on. They quickly made their way back to their room. Though they didn't have any homework, they were working on finding the truth behind the ghostly apparitions. Now that they were getting clarity piecing it all together, what do they do next?

Renton and Truman read to each other all night long while taking more notes. They concluded that the spirits were trying to show them something. They were both determined to find out what that something was all about and fix it.

First off, the fact that young Edward was revealing himself was indication to the boys that he was hiding something during this time in his life. It was clearly documented that he died an old man in this very manor. Because they identified him from the pictures, they just didn't understand. Renton looked at the clock and decided to call it a night. It was nearly midnight and they had to wake up at 7am. Truman was anxious as he knew the lights were going to be turned off. Every night just like clockwork the apparitions would appear. They said their goodnights and off to sleep the two boys drifted quickly and peacefully.

Truman began dreaming a dream that seemed so very real. He was on the edge of the cliff, standing overlooking the ocean. It was a nice fall day with lots of sunshine. He could smell the lavender from the gardens nearby. Suddenly, there were hands grabbing him in bed. They were stretching up from underneath his bed. The hands were long strange, pale, white, and grabbing at his body. Truman fighting off the unwanted hands felt a push and to no avail he began falling, hitting up against the sharp jagged cliffs and rocks below. He laid still paralyzed not able to move. He looked up towards the cliff where he once stood and there peering over the edge of it was young Edward. He was staring blankly at Truman as his limp body was being pulled by the ebbs of the oceans out into a sea of nothingness. Quickly Truman realized he was not in his own body that he was floating into the ocean. Or was he? Was he in his own body that had fallen from the cliff? Or was it young Elizabeth? One thing he was certain of was that it was Edward standing at the top of the cliff. He was sure that he had a scowl on his face as an evil laugh lingered echoing over the ocean. A soft mist of fog lingered in the air. All Truman could hear were waves crashing against the jagged boulders. Blackness was all around him.

Truman woke up in a sweat and crying. He couldn't contain himself. It seemed so real. The realization that poor little Elizabeth's life ended at the hands of her brother Edward. Truman didn't sleep well that night. He had a hard time getting the horrible fall that Elizabeth had endured out of his mind. It played repeatedly. To think this was just outside his window and all happened right here at Grey Cliff Manor was sickening. How did this happen, and no one knows? What was he to do with all the information that he had? This happened two hundred years ago or so. He could not wait to share what he had dreamed with Renton in the morning.

At the same time, Richard was standing at the door making his rounds and Truman had to share his dream with him. To Truman's astonishment Richard already knew.

"Well, I didn't really know for sure. It was rumored that young Edward was questioned for the accident. Nothing happened to him even though the police had reason to believe it was deliberate on Edward's part. It was well known that he witnessed his sister's accident. There was no further investigation since Mr. Appleton wanted the case closed and out of the news due to the nature of what had happened and the fact it would tarnish the Appleton's reputation. So, the case was closed and ruled as an accident," said Richard sadly.

"So basically, the Appleton's as well as the community really knew what happened and young Edward got away with murder?" asked Truman now in disbelief.

Just then, Renton woke up hearing what Richard and Truman were talking about.

"Unbelievable! That is so messed up!" said Renton. "There has to be something we can do!"

Richard sighed and shrugged his shoulders. He said that he didn't know what was able to be done hundreds of years later to make things right. He advised the boys to get back to sleep, quickly turned the lights off and shut the door as he made his way out going down

the long dark corridor.

CHAPTER NINE

FALL BREAK

Days, weeks went on and turned into months. There was always a chill in the air that came from the seasons changing. Fall had arrived and it was on the verge of winter. The air was always colder at Grey Cliff Manor, both inside and out.

The two boys had become closer to one another. Truman and Renton teamed up doing everything together from rooming, eating, academics, and even soccer. They had little interaction with the other students. Everyone seemed to have their own little clicks, and the two boys were just fine with the ways things were. The coming break would be the first time the two boys would be apart from one another since the school year began at Grey Cliff. There would be an entire week break, and Truman wondered what his parents would have in store for him. Renton looked forward to seeing his family and hoped that it would even snow. Maybe he would go sled riding with his two younger brothers. He was looking forward to putting up the Christmas tree and joining in the preparation of all the upcoming holiday festivities.

Renton finished packing his bags for the week ahead. He quickly straightened up his side of the room, which seemed to be in constant disarray ever since he showed up the first day. Due to his accident and his sprained ankle, he couldn't get as organized as he should have been. Thankfully, Truman helped him quite a bit with putting his things away. Renton was really going to miss his cousin when away. His parents would be there first thing in the morning to take him home. Truman had not heard anything about when his parents would be sending for him.

The two boys took an evening walk around the grounds just after dinner. The cold winds blew through their hair and they both bundled up in their warm coats. They pulled their scarves closer around their necks and the chill cut through to their bones. They walked toward the dining hall to join in with the other boys for hot coco and cinnamon rolls, a tasty after dinner treat. There was a raging fire in the huge fireplace and the two boys warmed themselves up quite nicely.

Outside the huge bay window, they could see the sun setting and there was a full moon rising in the horizon. Some called it a wolf moon, and you could hear the cries and howls of wolves in the faint distance. There was always a wind blowing through the drafty windows, and this night was no exception. You could feel the anticipation of the boys that were headed home to be with their families for Thanksgiving. There was also a deep feeling of remorse lingering in the air for those who were to stay behind. The school would indeed hold a nice feast for the boys that would be staying but it was no comparison to spending time at home with family. Luckily the two boys were not going to be staying behind.

They finished up their coco and headed up the grand stairway, down the long dark corridor. One thing that Renton would not miss while away was the creepy noises and unsettling visons of the apparitions that always showed up when the two boys were alone in their bedroom at night. There did not seem to be anything they could do about it and though it was terrifying they just had gotten used to it. The boys decided they would not share the paranormal experiences with their families due to the fact it wouldn't do them any good. Their parents would just scoff at it and chalk it up as rubbish.

Truman soon began to pack his bag. He methodically packed, not excited but rather out of routine. He knew there not anything to look forward to other than shopping with his parents in the hustle bustle, the busiest time of the year to be in New York City. It was nothing Truman wanted to do. He knew too well that they would end up staying for a good part of his week in a stuffy penthouse and eating in boring exorbitant restaurants. It was not something a typical thirteen-year-old boy called fun. Truman plopped on the bed and began reading a book. His reading light was on and the full moon shining through the window. The room was deafening quiet. Renton drifted off to sleep and Truman soon after falling asleep as well. All was quiet through the night, for a change. A cold chill continued to blow through the boy's room as they curled up snug in their covers for a good

night's rest.

CHAPTER TEN

DEPARTURE

Morning came quickly and Renton rose bright and early. He was eager to see his family and he began to get dressed. He dressed in layers with a nice green cardigan. It was the longest he had been away from his family and he somehow managed fine. Of course, it was due to the fact Truman was there with him, and it was quite the adventure. Looking over at Truman's bed he noticed that Truman had already made it. Not only was his bed made but his bags were gone as well.

Renton decided to carry his bags down to the foyer while waiting his parents to arrive. Quickly he headed for the dining hall to sit with Truman for breakfast. There was a lot of chatter in the air. Most everyone was excited for the fall break.

Renton scanned the room looking for Truman, but he couldn't find him. He didn't notice his bags in the foyer either. Renton was beginning to think that possibly Truman had already been picked up. A bit puzzled, Renton ate some French toast and drank some hot mint tea. He shuffled around cleaning up after himself and headed back out to the foyer. It was still early enough, around 10am and his parents would be arriving shortly. He sat on one of the loveseats in the foyer reading his book and biding his time. He was hoping to see Truman before he left for the week, but nevertheless they would be back here again in about a week. He had hoped that Truman could of went home with him for the break. The two boys had talked about it but neither got a chance to ask their parents. They were making plans for summer break and Renton was sure that his parents would allow him to spend the summer with them instead of being hauled from one country to the next. Truman hated all the travel, and though Renton's parents traveled as well, it was not quite as excessive.

Their fathers were brothers, and they were different as night and day. Though they both were both self-made and had a substantial amount of wealth, their views of what was important and family values seemed quite different. They seldom got together as families do, especially when their mother, also Renton and Truman's Nana passed away. It seemed to be a strain of sorts, but nothing was ever talked about. There just wasn't much engagement between the two brothers.

Renton was ecstatic about being reacquainted with his cousin. He looked forward to spending time with Truman in the future. The two of them were more like brothers than cousins. Even though they had barely known one another growing up, that one summer at their Nanas five years ago really brought them together. Summertime at their Nana's was quite memorable. It was no surprise to either of the boys that they picked up where they left off with ease.

The morning came and went. Still Renton remained in the foyer reading his book. Grey Cliff Manor was dwindling down as more and more boys were leaving. The skies began to darken, and Renton looked at his watch. Where could his parents be? Why are they taking so long, Renton wondered to himself. He looked around and everyone had seemed to vanish. All the luggage that was packed in the foyer was now gone. Renton began to get nervous and decided to look for the school master. Maybe he would call for his parents. He edged his way towards the directory and rang the night bell. The silence of Grey Cliff was stifling, and the air was thick. Renton sat in the now darkened foyer. He heard faint footsteps from around the corridor and was hoping it would be the school master. Renton began to feel a dread creep up on him as though something was terribly wrong. He couldn't shake the feeling. He began imagining that the school master would come with a horrible message that something had happened to his parents. He was frightened that they were in a terrible car crash or something similar.

Outside the window he thought he saw a glimpse of Truman walking swiftly passed the window. He was heading towards the cliff. The wind through the foyer was howling eerily. He grabbed his coat and ran outside after his cousin. He yelled Truman's name, but the boy did not look back at him. He continued the journey to out near the cliff.

The night skies were lit up by electricity as the thunder began from beyond the fields. You could feel the rain coming. The thickness of the air was dense. Renton continued calling for Truman, as he ran toward the cliff where his cousin was headed. Out of the corner of Renton's eye he saw two other figures. One was of another boy and one of a small child. The wind was wild and so were the skies. The sky was lighting up like nothing he had ever seen.

Renton stopped dead in his tracks as he watched the small child being pushed from the cliff. Just a few steps away the other boy turned his head towards Renton with a sinister look in his eyes. The loud sinister laughter

coming from the strange boy's mouth was

deafening. Truman stood on the edge of the

cliff. The strange boy then pushed him off as

he did with the small child just minutes ago.

Truman was screaming Renton's name.

Renton felt his heart stop and he couldn't

breathe. The winds encircled him, and he fell

to his knees. He could not make sense of what

he had just seen right before his eyes.

After a few seconds Renton turned

around to run inside for help. There, stood

Truman wet, broken, pale white and dead. He

was now an apparition the same as the others.

"I don't understand," whispered Renton.

"Neither do I," replied Truman. He had no expression on his face. It was only bruised broken and pale. The school master then showed up. He was also now looking pale white and dead.

"It is time to come inside boys and get dried off," he said.

Just as the two boys began to follow the school master into the manor, the small child began running alongside of the two boys.

"I want to get warm too," the child said softly. "And I would like some coco."

Renton was not sure what was happening, but one thing he did know now, was that none of them were ever leaving Grey Cliff Manor. There would be no one picking up him or Truman. The two boys entered the foyer. The fire was blazing. The winds howled throughout Grey Cliff Manor.

The End

The Author

D.A. Wysong is an Author of 11 Children's books. She is currently working on a new series based on urban myths and legends. The new series is entitled Creeper Ceepers. D.A. Wysong is also a Screenwriter as well as a Novelist. She currently resides in Bellevue Kentucky and keeps her muses alive through travel, art, music, and researching. Her favorite genre is the paranormal.

The Illustrator (cover)

Jorge Tracheta currently resides in Mexico.

He enjoys working with horror themed art.

The **Creeper Ceepers** Series One

Book **One** – The Haunting of Grey Cliff Manor

Book **Two** – The Tale of the Greenwich Werewolf

Book **Three** – The Doll Maker

Book **Four** – Trilogy of Terror – Scarecrows, Black Eyed Kids & the Haunted Pumpkin Patch

Book **Five** – Trilogy of Haunted Yuletide Tales

Book **Six** – The Creepiest Cemetery Ever

Book **Seven** – Dark Sisters of the Craft

Book **Eight** – The Haunted Road Trip

Book **Nine** – Soul Suckers & the Anatomy of a Cell Phone

Book **Ten** – Wendigos in the Woods

Book **Eleven** – Just One Shot

Book **Twelve** – Killer Clowns & the Crazed You-Tuber

Book **Thirteen** – Vampire Darkness in the French Quarter

Other Books by D.A. Wysong

Before Time Was

Tippy, Torry & the Mouse

A Nishy Pop Tale

A Rainy-Day Birthday

101 Chicken Pox & Lots of Weasels

So You Want a Baby Alligator & Lots of Other Animals

Holding Zaylei

You Can Call Me Pickle Puss

The Song of Kenzie Bear

Shaun Lee's Super-Duper Trip to the Zoo

Scuba Diving with Kayden Aaron

Astrology 101- A Child's Guide to the Stars and Planets

Made in United States
Orlando, FL
14 April 2022

16832752R10065